The Just Desserts Club

By Johanna Hurwitz

The Adventures of Ali Baba Bernstein
Aldo Applesauce
Aldo Ice Cream
Aldo Peanut Butter
Ali Baba Bernstein, Lost and Found
Baseball Fever
Birthday Surprises: Ten Great Stories to Unwrap
Busybody Nora
Class Clown
Class President
The Cold & Hot Winter
DeDe Takes Charge!
The Down & Up Fall
"E" Is for Elisa
Elisa in the Middle
Even Stephen
Ever-Clever Elisa
Faraway Summer
The Hot & Cold Summer
Hurray for Ali Baba Bernstein
Hurricane Elaine

The Law of Gravity
A Llama in the Family
Llama in the Library
Make Room for Elisa
Much Ado About Aldo
New Neighbors for Nora
New Shoes for Silvia
Nora and Mrs. Mind-Your-Own-Business
Once I Was a Plum Tree
Ozzie on His Own
The Rabbi's Girls
Rip-Roaring Russell
Roz and Ozzie
Russell and Elisa
Russell Rides Again
Russell Sprouts
School's Out
School Spirit
Spring Break
Starting School
Superduper Teddy
Teacher's Pet
Tough-Luck Karen
The Up & Down Spring
A Word to the Wise: And Other Proverbs
Yellow Blue Jay

JOHANNA HURWITZ

Illustrated by **KAREN DUGAN**

MORROW JUNIOR BOOKS
NEW YORK

Published by Morrow Junior Books
a division of William Morrow and Company, Inc.
1350 Avenue of the Americas, New York, NY 10019
www.williammorrow.com

Printed in the United States of America.

1 3 5 7 9 10 8 6 4 2

Library of Congress Cataloging-in-Publication Data
Hurwitz, Johanna.
The just desserts club / Johanna Hurwitz.
p. cm.
Summary: Sixth grader Cricket finds just the right dessert to bake for school events during the year. Includes recipes for Zucchini "Apple" Crisp, No Bake Orange Balls, and Mystery Ingredient Chocolate Cake.
ISBN 0-688-16266-5
[1. Desserts—Fiction. 2. Baking—Fiction. 3. Schools—Fiction.] I. Title.
PZ7.H9574Ju 1999 [Fic]—dc21 99-19039 CIP

Once again for Caroline Feller Bauer,
who's been sharing recipes with me for
forty years. At least two of Cricket's
cookie recipes came from her.

Contents

THREE

FOUR

Recipe for a Good Time

Ingredients

1 group of friends—any number, girls and boys
large amount of cooperation—as many
parts as there are participants
1 part sense of humor
2 parts sharing
2 parts compromise
1 kitchen and 1 parent to oversee use of stove,
sharp utensils, and general activities

Cooking Directions

- Wash hands before touching food.
- Take turns doing all activities.
- Follow directions carefully. Mix all ingredients listed above. If something doesn't turn out as planned, don't blame anyone. You can always learn from your mistakes.
- Clean up kitchen while food is cooking.
- Enjoy the results!

ONE

The Zucchini Houdini

Cricket Kaufman had a secret. She couldn't admit it to her friends because they would think she was weird. But the truth was, she wished the summer vacation were over. Cricket loved school. She liked her teachers and *most* of her classmates. She even enjoyed doing homework assignments and the challenge of taking tests. So when summer vacation stretched on and on for two full months, she became miserable. She began counting the days until school would reopen and sixth grade would begin.

Someday in the future, when Cricket was the first woman president of the United States, one of the first laws she'd make would concern school vacations. She'd make a law that instead of having all of July and August off from school, four days of school would be followed by three-day weekends all year long.

This summer had started out pretty great. Cricket had gone to Washington, D.C., with her mother and her classmate Sara Jane Cushman. After returning from the trip, Cricket went swimming at the community pool and enjoyed backyard picnics with Sara Jane and her other best friend, Zoe Mitchell. Then in mid-August, both Sara Jane and Zoe had gone away on family vacations, and Cricket was alone.

To pass the time, she read many books, including twelve biographies of American presidents—but it turned out that most of them had led lives that were just as dull as hers. Every day started to feel exactly the same. Why, her mother had even prepared zucchini for supper three nights in a row! That was another law President Cricket Kaufman would have to make: No more zucchini!

Cricket didn't actually dislike zucchini, but three nights in a row was too much. It was all because her father had come home from work with an enormous bag of the long green vegetables.

"Bob Eversham says his garden is exploding with zucchini this year," Mr. Kaufman had reported to his wife. He put the brown paper bag down on the kitchen counter. Mrs. Kaufman removed a total of nine zucchini.

"How wonderful!" Cricket's mother had exclaimed.

So on Monday night the family ate steamed zucchini with their chicken cutlets.

On Tuesday Mrs. Butler, who lived across the street from the Kaufman family, dropped by with a large plastic grocery bag. "I've just returned from visiting my sister in Delaware," she said. "She wouldn't let me leave without some vegetables from her garden. I'm keeping the tomatoes that she gave me, but I thought you could use these." The bag was filled with zucchini.

When Mrs. Kaufman had finished preparing zucchini in tomato sauce for that evening's supper, Cricket noticed that they were now down to eleven zucchini in the refrigerator. But a little later, her father returned home from work with a second bag of them from his coworker.

"At this rate, we won't have room for even a quart of milk," said Mrs. Kaufman as she stuffed several more zucchini into the refrigerator. The six zucchini that she couldn't fit inside remained on the kitchen counter. It looked like the Kaufmans would be eating zucchini until Halloween.

Since Cricket's mother knew only two ways to prepare zucchini—steamed or with a tomato sauce—on Wednesday Cricket was faced with eating the steamed vegetable for the second time in three days. She shuddered.

"I'm tired of eating zucchini every night," Cricket complained.

"I understand how you feel," said Mrs. Kaufman. "But we can't let this fresh produce go to waste. So you'll just have to pretend that you're eating something else for the next few days."

That's ridiculous, Cricket thought. How can you eat zucchini and pretend that it's something else? It was at that moment that Cricket made an executive decision. She would figure out another way to cook those vegetables. She finally had something new to do with her time!

On Thursday morning she headed off to the public library. She returned the biographies of John Tyler and Calvin Coolidge and then, instead of looking for another life story of a former American president, she headed for the cookbook area.

That's when Cricket made one of the most amazing discoveries since gold was found in

California back in the nineteenth century. In addition to finding recipes for frying, roasting, and baking zucchini, she learned that the vegetable could also be used as an ingredient in several desserts.

Cricket copied some of the most interesting recipes into the notebook she had brought with her, and then she started for home. She could hardly wait to try one of the new recipes.

As she was hurrying down the street, Cricket met two of her friends from school, Lucas Cott and Julio Sanchez. They had their skateboards under their arms, and Lucas was carrying a plastic bag of marshmallows.

"I thought you were at sleep-away camp," Cricket said to Lucas.

"I was. For three weeks. But now I'm home again." He looked at Cricket, who was holding her notebook in her left hand. "Don't tell me you're doing homework already! School doesn't start for another two weeks."

"I'm not doing homework," Cricket said.

"What were you writing in that notebook?" Julio asked.

"I was doing some private research," Cricket retorted. Why did Julio and Lucas have to know about everything? "What are you doing here with that bag of marshmallows?" Cricket asked Lucas.

"We just bought them," Lucas explained. "I'm going to show Julio how to be a *chubby bunny.* It's a game we played at camp."

"I never heard of it," said Cricket.

"Me neither," Julio said. "But it sounds like fun. All you have to do is stuff your mouth with marshmallows. The one who can put the most inside is the winner."

Lucas ripped open the bag and pulled out a fistful of marshmallows. "Start counting," he said.

Cricket and Julio kept score as Lucas stuck one marshmallow after another into his mouth. When he reached eight, he couldn't fit another one in.

"Boy, do you look stupid," Cricket told Lucas.

When Lucas tried to protest, two of the marshmallows popped out of his mouth and landed on the ground. He began chewing the ones still in his mouth. "It's fun," he said in a voice choked by the contents of his mouth. "Especially if you like marshmallows."

"I like everything," said Julio, reaching for the

plastic bag. "Let's see what I can do. I bet I can beat your record."

Julio managed to push nine soft white pieces into his open jaws.

"You don't look like a chubby bunny. You look like a hamster," Cricket proclaimed. She was remembering the class pet from back in first grade.

"Do you want a turn?" Lucas asked, offering the bag.

"I'll just take one to eat," said Cricket, and turned to walk away. It might be fun to see how many marshmallows she could fit into her mouth, but she certainly wouldn't do it out on the street, where anyone could walk by and see her looking so ridiculous.

"Where are you going now?" Lucas wanted to know.

"I'm going home to bake some—" Cricket stopped herself from finishing the sentence. "I'm going to cook a surprise. I bet you'd never be able to guess what mystery ingredient is in it."

"Sure we could," said Julio, who was licking the powdered sugar from his lips after swallowing all the marshmallows that had been in his mouth.

"I eat everything, and I always know what I'm chewing on." He grinned at Cricket. "What do you want to bet that I can guess whatever your mystery ingredient is?"

"If I win the bet, you have to give me a prize," said Cricket. "And if you win, I'll give you something."

"Like what?" Lucas asked suspiciously. He wasn't certain he wanted to taste anything Cricket cooked up. Once last spring he'd eaten a cupcake that she'd made, and it had been pretty awful.

"Wait and see," Cricket told Lucas. She wasn't worried about having to give him or Julio anything. There was no way they'd guess the mystery ingredient.

"Come over to my house at three o'clock," she told the boys.

"Okay," Julio agreed. "See you later."

Back home, Mrs. Kaufman was amused by her daughter's research. "Which of these recipes do you want to make?" she asked.

"This one," Cricket replied, pointing to the pie recipe. If it tasted as good as it looked in the cookbook, it would certainly trick Lucas and Julio.

Mrs. Kaufman studied the recipe. Luckily, they had all of the ingredients in the house. As soon as lunch was over and Cricket's little sister, Monica, was in bed for her afternoon nap, Cricket and her mother began working together.

By three o'clock Monica was wide-awake and playing on the backyard swings. Cricket was sitting on a lawn chair, keeping an eye on her sister. A spicy, cinnamony odor, like apple pie, was coming from inside the house. Cricket could hardly wait for the two boys to arrive. She just knew this was one bet with Lucas Cott that she was guaranteed to win.

Suddenly Cricket heard Lucas's voice. "Stop that," he ordered someone.

Cricket ran to the front of the house and was dismayed to see that Lucas and Julio were not alone. They were accompanied by Lucas's younger brothers, Marcus and Marius.

"Why did you bring *them*?" Cricket demanded.

"My mother said I had to take care of them. A filling fell out of her tooth at lunchtime, and she had to make an emergency appointment with the dentist. She didn't think Marcus and Marius would sit still in the dentist's office while they waited for her."

"We never sit still," said Marius proudly.

"We never sit still. We never *stand* still," said

Marcus. He jumped up and down to prove his point.

"Well, you'd better sit still in my house," Cricket warned the boys. "Come on inside." She called to Monica, and the little girl came running.

"Who are you?" Monica asked Lucas's brothers.

"Marcus."

"Marius."

"How do you know which of you is which?" Monica asked them. It was a logical question for a three-year-old. Lucas's brothers were identical twins.

"I just do," said Marius.

Mrs. Kaufman greeted everyone. "This is turning into a real party," she said as she took plates and glasses from the cupboard.

"Boy, that apple pie sure smells good," Julio commented as they all sat down around the kitchen table.

"Wait till you taste it," said Cricket, smiling mysteriously.

"I want a big piece," demanded Marcus.

"Me too," said Marius.

"Me too," said Monica.

"Not me," said Lucas. "I'll just take a little bit." There was something about the expression on Cricket's face that made him even more suspicious than he was before.

Mrs. Kaufman poured glasses of milk for everyone. Then she cut big and small slices of the pie.

"Oh, man," said Julio, chewing his first mouthful of the pie. "This is the greatest."

"More," demanded Marcus as he stuffed pie into his mouth.

"Careful, Marius," said Mrs. Kaufman, looking at him. "You almost knocked your glass of milk off of the table."

"No, I didn't," said Marius. "You mean Marcus."

Mrs. Kaufman turned her head from one twin to the other. At that moment one of them did knock over his glass of milk. The milk spilled onto the table and dribbled down onto the floor. Some of it landed on Marcus's bare knee.

"The milk tickles," he announced cheerfully.

"Let me wash you up," said Mrs. Kaufman, taking Marcus away from the table.

"I want to watch," said Marius, following his twin.

"Me too," added Monica. "I'm a big girl. I don't

spill anymore," she told Lucas's brothers.

"So what," said Marius. "We're bigger than you. We're going to be in kindergarten."

"Spilling is fun," said Marcus as he followed Cricket's mother to the bathroom.

There was one slice of pie left. Julio looked at it longingly.

"You can have it," Cricket told him. "But first you have to guess what the mystery ingredient is. And if you can't get it, I win the bet."

"Apples?" suggested Lucas.

"Nope."

"Pears?" guessed Julio.

"Nope."

"Only one more guess each," said Cricket. "Otherwise you could go through everything they sell at the supermarket until you accidentally guess the right thing."

Lucas rubbed his tongue around in his mouth. "Peaches?" he asked.

"Last guess," said Cricket, looking at Julio.

Julio licked his lips. He looked around the kitchen for a clue. "It sure tastes like apple pie," he said. "But if it isn't apples then it must be, be, be . . ." His eyes landed on the row of zucchini sitting on the kitchen counter. "What do you call those green things over there?" he asked Lucas.

Lucas turned to see where Julio was pointing. "You mean those vegetables? That's zucchini."

"That's it, then," said Julio. "I bet you made this pie out of zucchini."

"You're just making a guess." said Cricket. "You don't *know* what I used, do you?"

Julio shrugged his shoulders. "Okay," he sighed. "What did you use?"

"Zucchini!" Cricket called out triumphantly. She was delighted that she'd outwitted both boys.

"But that's what I said," Julio insisted. "I said zucchini."

"You said it, but you didn't *mean* it. It was just a wild guess. You didn't think you were right. You didn't even know what they were until Lucas told you."

"It doesn't matter," argued Lucas. "He said it, and he was right. He won the bet."

"That's right," said Julio smugly. "Now you have to give me a prize."

"You'd never have guessed if my mother had put those zucchini inside the refrigerator," Cricket protested.

"You must be a magician to make a pie out of a

vegetable like that. It doesn't taste like a vegetable at all," Julio said.

"You're a zucchini Houdini!" Lucas admitted.

"I could Houdini zucchini into a lot of other things," Cricket bragged. "I found out how to make brownies and cookies and other desserts with zucchini when I was in the library this morning."

"No kidding," said Lucas. "Is that what you were doing? I wish my mother would cook vegetables that way. Vegetables for dessert. I like that idea."

"Do you want to come over tomorrow and help me cook one of the other recipes?" Cricket suggested. "But only if Lucas leaves Marcus and Marius at home. You can't cook and baby-sit at the same time."

"That's okay," said Lucas. "My mother doesn't lose a filling from her teeth every day."

"That's a great plan," Julio said.

"Yeah," Lucas agreed. "Cooking would be fun. But don't forget: just desserts."

Soon it was time for Lucas, Marcus, Marius, and Julio to go home.

"Hey," Lucas said to Cricket suddenly. "I have a

food riddle for you. I heard it at camp: What food is this? You throw away the outside, cook the inside, eat the outside, and throw away the inside?"

"That doesn't make sense," Cricket complained.

"It does when you know the answer," said Lucas. "Give up?"

"I do," said Julio. "What is it?"

"An ear of corn," said Lucas, proud to have stumped both friends.

"I would have guessed it you'd given me more time," Cricket argued.

"No, you wouldn't. No one ever guesses the answer."

"Wait a minute," Julio interrupted. "Aren't you forgetting something? I'm supposed to get a prize from you for guessing about the zucchini. Remember?"

Cricket *did* remember, but it didn't seem fair. Julio had made a lucky guess. Well, he'd get his "just desserts" all right!

"Wait outside," she told the boys. "I'll bring Julio his prize in one minute."

Lucas, Marcus, Marius, and Julio waited in front of Cricket's house. "I never won a prize before," said Julio, eager to see what he'd get.

Cricket came out and handed Julio a paper bag. "Here's your prize," she told him.

Julio quickly opened the bag and let out a groan. Inside were two large green zucchini. But there were still fourteen zucchini left at the Kaufman house. Plenty for cooking with the next day.

Zucchini "Apple" Crisp

Ingredients for Pie Filling

8 cups peeled and sliced zucchini (three or four zucchini, depending on size)
⅔ cup lemon juice
1 cup white sugar
1 teaspoon cinnamon
½ teaspoon nutmeg

Topping for Pie

¾ stick of butter or margarine, at room temperature
½ cup oatmeal
½ cup flour
½ cup light brown sugar
1 ready-to-use piecrust

Cooking Directions

• Preheat oven to 350 degrees.

• Cook zucchini and lemon juice in a saucepan on top of the stove until tender—about 30 minutes. During last 10 minutes add sugar, cinnamon, and nutmeg, and stir everything together.

• While zucchini is cooking, mix all the topping ingredients in a large bowl. This works best and also is most fun when done with your fingers, but be sure to wash your hands thoroughly first!

• Pour zucchini mixture into ready-to-use piecrust.

• Add topping. Bake for 30 minutes.

• Allow to cool before eating.

• Fool your friends by telling them that this is an apple pie!

Brownie Surprise Cake

(The surprise is that it is made with zucchini.)

Ingredients

1 stick butter or margarine, at room temperature
½ cup canola or corn oil
1 ¾ cups white sugar
1 teaspoon vanilla
2 eggs
½ cup plain yogurt
½ cup cocoa powder
½ teaspoon baking powder
1 teaspoon baking soda
½ teaspoon salt
2 cups flour
2 cups unpeeled grated zucchini (about two zucchini)

½ cup chocolate chips
½ cup chopped walnuts (optional)

Cooking Directions

- Preheat oven to 350 degrees.

- In a large bowl, mix butter or margarine together with oil. Add eggs and vanilla. Beat until smooth.

- Add yogurt.

- In a separate bowl, combine flour, cocoa, baking powder, baking soda, and salt, and stir into the wet batter.

- Add zucchini, chocolate chips, and nuts (if you don't like nuts, you can leave them out). Stir until everything is blended together.

- Pour batter into a greased and floured 9-inch-by-13-inch baking pan or a tube pan.

- Bake for an hour. Test for doneness by sticking a wooden toothpick into cake. If it comes out clean, you will know that the brownies are done. If not, allow to bake another few minutes and test again.

- Cool before removing from pan.

Zucchini Bread

This recipe makes two loaves. You can always give one to a friend or wrap one in aluminum foil and freeze for another day. To make only one loaf, use one whole egg plus one egg yolk, and use half of all of the other ingredients.

Ingredients

3 eggs
1 cup canola or corn oil
2 ½ cups white sugar
2 cups grated zucchini, unpeeled
3 teaspoons vanilla
3 cups flour
1 teaspoon baking soda
½ teaspoon baking powder
3 teaspoons cinnamon
½ teaspoon salt

chopped walnuts or pecans and raisins
(optional)

Cooking Directions

- Preheat oven to 325 degrees.

- Combine eggs, oil, sugar, zucchini, and vanilla in a large bowl. Beat using an electric mixer (if you have one—if not, use an eggbeater and a lot of muscle).

- Add flour, baking soda, baking powder, cinnamon, salt, and, if you want them, nuts and raisins.

- Mix well. Batter will be runny.

- Pour into two greased and floured loaf pans.

- Bake for about one hour. Use a toothpick to test for doneness.

- Cool in pan for about ten minutes. Turn pan upside down and loaf will fall out.

Zucchini Cookies

Ingredients

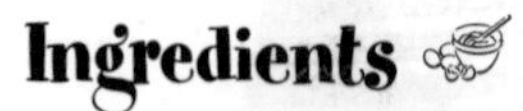

¾ stick butter or margarine, at room temperature
¾ cup light brown sugar
1 egg
½ teaspoon vanilla
grated rind of one orange
1 ½ cups grated zucchini, unpeeled
1 ¾ cups flour
½ teaspoon baking soda
½ teaspoon salt
1 ½ cups granola cereal
½ cup chocolate or butterscotch chips

Cooking Directions

- Preheat oven to 350 degrees.
- Mix butter or margarine with sugar. Add egg, vanilla, and grated orange rind. Add zucchini.
- Into this mixture add flour, baking soda, salt, granola, and chips.
- When all is mixed together, drop by spoonfuls onto an ungreased baking sheet. Leave spaces between cookies, as they will spread when they cook.
- Bake for 12 to 15 minutes.
- Allow to cool for a minute or two before removing with a spatula.

TWO

Cooking Up a Plan

Sixth grade was even better than Cricket had ever imagined. First of all, she was together once again with all her old friends—Zoe, Sara Jane, Lucas, and Julio. But the best thing about sixth grade was being part of the oldest group at the Edison-Armstrong School. This had its privileges, as well as its responsibilities—which suited Cricket just fine, because she had always felt a little more grown-up than everyone else.

So Cricket was especially excited when their sixth-grade teacher, Mrs. Cheechia, told her class that they were going to run the annual clothing drive. Cricket remembered contributing her old snow boots to the drive the previous year. Now she found herself going around the school and reminding the students to bring in warm clothing, which would be donated to the homeless shelter in town. Since Cricket loved telling people what to do, this was a job she really enjoyed. No wonder the sixth graders collected more clothing this year than ever before.

It was a bit of a letdown when the clothing drive ended. "Now we should do something else," Cricket suggested to her teacher.

"What do you have in mind?" Mrs. Cheechia asked. For once, Cricket didn't have an answer.

"How about a food drive?" said Julio. "It's no good being warm if you're feeling hungry. Let's collect food to give away."

"I wish someone would collect something for *me* to eat," Lucas called out. "I slept so late this morning, I hardly had any breakfast."

"It serves you right," scolded Cricket. "You should get up on time, like I do."

"Never mind." Mrs. Cheechia hushed the students. "Let's see a show of hands. How many think they'd like to take part in a food drive?"

Every hand in the class went up. Even Lucas Cott forgot his own stomach for the moment and agreed it was a good plan.

"We should bring in canned goods and things that won't spoil," said Zoe.

"What kind of things?" asked Arthur.

"Think for a minute," Mrs. Cheechia instructed.

"What comes in a package and stays fresh without refrigeration?"

"Wrapped elephants," Lucas called out, and everyone laughed.

Mrs. Cheechia sighed. "Lucas Cott, sometimes I feel like wrapping *you* up and putting you in a package."

Lucas would be fresh whether wrapped or unwrapped, Cricket thought.

The students suggested types of food that would not spoil: pasta, rice, dried beans, and cookies.

"What about bread?" asked Arthur.

"No, no," Cricket called out, forgetting to raise her hand. "Bread would get stale or even moldy after a few days."

"You could always make toast out of stale bread," replied Arthur, defending his suggestion.

"You could make penicillin out of moldy bread," shouted Lucas. He smiled triumphantly when he got another laugh.

Mrs. Cheechia ignored Lucas. "Think before you bring anything in," she reminded her students. "Ask yourself if it could sit on a shelf in the back of our classroom for a couple of weeks without going bad."

"Could we make announcements on the public-address system?" asked Cricket. She had enjoyed doing that for the clothing drive. In fact, as she sat in her seat she suddenly got a great idea: Rhymed slogans would make the messages stick in people's heads. She opened her notebook and started scribbling some potential announcements:

Ask your Aunt Milly for a can of chili.
Will you please bring a can of peas.
It's not too rash to bring corned beef hash.
We'll give a whoop if you donate a can of soup.

Mrs. Cheechia thought the announcements were a great idea. And over the next couple of weeks, Cricket was pleased to hear students repeating the rhymes she and her classmates read every morning over the PA system. The food contributions began piling up as a result.

Cricket's mother donated a brand-new jar of strawberry jam, two cans of sardines, and a bottle of ketchup. Cricket felt sorry for the people who would get these contributions. What kind of meal would that make? Sardines with ketchup and strawberry jam!

That's when Cricket got another idea. "If we

collected money, as well as food, the needy people could go out and buy fresh things too. They could get bread and butter, or cheese or meat."

"That's true, Cricket," Mrs. Cheechia agreed. "If anyone would like to donate money from their allowance or their savings, I will collect it for this cause. However, I don't want you to ask your parents for money. This should be a student effort. Perhaps a few of you could think of ways to raise some money."

"I know how we could get loads of money," Julio announced.

"Loads of money?" called out Lucas. "What are we going to do? Dig for gold out in the school yard?"

"No," said Julio. "We could collect soda cans and get the nickel deposit on each of them. I saw two cans in the street on my way to school this morning. I bet we could find a ton of cans."

"My father drinks a can of beer with his supper sometimes," a girl called out. "You get a nickel back on beer cans too."

"All right, kids. Any money we can collect will be a bonus," said Mrs. Cheechia. "I'm delighted that you have all gotten into the spirit of giving. Bring in any money that you make collecting cans, and we'll get gift certificates to be used at the supermarket."

Cricket thought about Julio's plan. Doing the math in her head, she realized that she and her classmates would have to find a hundred cans in order to earn five dollars.

"There's got to be a better way to earn money," she told Julio at lunchtime.

"Trust me," Julio replied. "Tomorrow's Saturday. If we go out together, we'll find a zillion cans."

Julio made it sound as if the streets were covered with empty cans, Cricket thought. She was certain they wouldn't find enough to make much money. But on the other hand, if Zoe and Sara Jane were going along with Lucas and Julio, she didn't want to be left out.

So the next morning she met up with her friends as planned. Lucas had brought along a wagon that belonged to his little brothers. "This will hold a lot of cans," he said optimistically.

"We'll need it to get the cans to the supermarket," Julio commented.

"First we have to *find* the cans," Cricket reminded everyone.

The five friends walked along the street with Lucas in the rear, pulling the old wagon. The wagon already contained two cans that Lucas had brought from home.

"How come I always see cans in the street when I'm not looking for them?" Sara Jane wondered aloud.

The streets were amazingly clean. Most people in the neighborhood had even raked and swept up the autumn leaves, collecting them neatly in large plastic bags.

Suddenly Lucas gave a shout. "There's one!" he called. All five kids ran toward the lone can, which was resting against the curb. Julio picked it up and threw it into the wagon.

"Wow!" said Cricket sarcastically. "Now we've made fifteen cents!"

"Believe me, we're going to make money before the day is over," Julio said.

"I *don't* believe you," Cricket said. "Why don't we have a bake sale? Then we'd really make money."

"When we had the bake sale at school last year, it was a lot of fun," Sara Jane remembered.

"Yeah. But it takes too long to bake things," Julio replied. "You'll spend all day cooking, and there won't be any time to sell the stuff."

"I know lots of easy recipes that don't take a

long time to fix," said Cricket. "I'll explain them if you guys decide to drop this silly hunt-the-can plan of yours and agree to have a bake sale instead. Let's take a vote. How many think we should have a bake sale?"

Even though she wasn't in school, Cricket raised her hand up in the air. Zoe and Sara Jane raised their hands up too. Lucas and Julio kept their hands at their sides.

"See. My plan wins," Cricket said triumphantly.

"So go have a bake sale," Lucas said. "Julio and I are going to collect cans. We don't need you."

"We'll earn more than you," Zoe warned the boys.

"Says who?" Lucas wanted to know.

"We do," said Cricket as she and Sara Jane and Zoe turned to leave the boys.

"Come to my house," Zoe invited. "I know my mom will let us do some cooking."

"Okay," Cricket agreed. She was pleased to have won the girls over to her point of view. She couldn't wait to tell them about the no-bake cookies that she knew how to make.

Cricket, Sara Jane, and Zoe, with a little assistance from Zoe's older sister, Halley, spent the next couple of hours cooking up some treats to sell.

Cricket saw an unopened box of vanilla wafers in the cupboard and used them for a recipe she knew. Halley taught the girls how to make another type of treat. They looked through Zoe's mother's cookbooks and found still another recipe that would be quick and easy to prepare.

They were so busy working in the kitchen that Zoe's mother offered to phone and order a pizza for their lunch. It was a good thing, because all the counter space was filled with plates of cookies. The sink was overflowing with dirty bowls and utensils. There was no room or time for meal preparation.

When lunch was over, the girls carried a folding table out to the street. "Let's set it up at the corner," Cricket suggested. "More people pass by that way."

It took more effort to transport everything to the corner, but it was worth it. Zoe insisted they needed to put a tablecloth on the table. And then they needed to bring out the trays with the things for sale.

"Too bad Lucas isn't here with the wagon," Sara Jane observed. "We could use it now."

"I wonder how much money they're making," Zoe said.

Bake Sale

"Not much," said Cricket.

Because it was a lovely autumn day, many people were outside. Some adults were working in their yards, two teenage boys were washing a car, and several young children were out on their bikes. It didn't take long for the table of baked goods to attract attention.

Zoe got an idea and ran back to her house. She returned carrying a half gallon of milk and some paper cups.

"Milk and two cookies are fifty cents," she announced.

"That's equal to *ten* empty cans!" Cricket said happily as she poured milk into cups for two little girls whose mother brought them—their first customers.

Before long there were many others waiting in line. The guys washing the car came over and bought thirty-five cents' worth of cookies.

"Don't you want to buy some milk?" asked Cricket.

"Naw," said one of them. "We've got some soda to drink." He pointed to two cans resting on the curb near the car.

"Keep an eye on the cans," Zoe whispered to her friends. "We'll show Lucas and Julio that we can sell cookies and collect empty cans at the same time."

Just as the rush of customers was over, Lucas and Julio came along the street. Lucas was still pulling the wagon, but there was nothing in it.

"Did you turn in your three cans?" Cricket asked.

"We turned in a whole lot more than three," said Julio.

"We found a man who had a garage full of cans. He said we could take them all and keep the deposit," Lucas said proudly. "He was going to do it himself, but he never got around to it. So when he heard we were going to give the money to charity, he offered them to us. He said it would probably be worth the effort."

"Well, was it?" asked Cricket.

"Was it what?" Julio responded.

"Worth the effort? How much did you make?"

"There sure were a lot of cans," Lucas remarked. "We had to make three separate trips to the supermarket because there were so many of them that they couldn't all fit in the wagon at once."

Julio put his hand in his pocket and pulled out several dollars. He started counting. "Seven dollars and thirty-five cents," he said.

"How many cans was that?" Sara Jane wanted to know.

"One hundred and forty seven," said Lucas and Cricket simultaneously. They were both good at math.

"That's an awful lot of soda and beer," said Zoe.

"How much did you make?" asked Julio.

Zoe counted up the bills and loose change. She gasped. "I don't believe it."

"Did we make *that* much money?" asked Cricket, pleased that her plan had been so successful.

"We made exactly seven dollars and thirty-five cents," Zoe replied.

"Hey. We both made the same amount," said Julio, smiling. He reached for a cookie that was on the tray in front of him and stuffed it into his mouth. "These are really good," he said, and he reached for another.

"Do you want some milk?" asked Cricket sweetly.

"Sure," said Julio. He gulped down the cup of milk his classmate poured for him.

"What about me?" asked Lucas. "Don't I get any? I worked pretty hard too."

"Sure," said Zoe. She handed Lucas a cup of milk and offered him a choice of cookies.

She looked at Cricket and Sara Jane, trying hard not to smile. Only when Lucas had drained his cup of milk and finished his cookies did anyone speak.

"You owe us a dollar," said Cricket with delight.

"A dollar? What for?" asked Lucas.

"Did you think we were standing here just giving this stuff away?" she asked him. "This bake sale is to raise money to buy food for the needy. Two cookies and a cup of milk cost fifty cents."

"But if we pay you with the money we made from the cans, we won't have as much to turn in at school."

"And we'll have earned more than you!" said Cricket smugly. There was a huge grin on her face.

"But it will all go to help the people who are hungry," Sara Jane reminded the boys.

"That's right," agreed Lucas. "I'm feeling pretty hungry now myself. In fact, I'm starving. Can you throw in an extra cookie or two?"

"Sure, help yourself," Cricket agreed. Now that

they had triumphed over the boys, she could afford to be generous. "Let's all finish them up," she suggested to her friends. And before long, the bake sale was completely sold out—even though not another penny was earned.

Sara Jane remembered the two empty soda cans at the edge of the sidewalk near the freshly washed car. She ran to get them and gave one to Julio and one to Lucas. "You can turn these in for another ten cents," she told them.

And that's why on Monday morning Mrs. Cheechia received an envelope with fourteen dollars and eighty cents. It was the combined effort of five students who had cooked up two plans—and some cookies as well.

No-Bake Orange Balls

Ingredients

1 twelve-ounce box of vanilla wafers, crushed
1 pound of confectioners' sugar
1 stick of butter or margarine, at room temperature
1 six-ounce can frozen orange juice concentrate
1 bag shredded coconut

Cooking Directions

• Mix butter and sugar together thoroughly.

• Add juice concentrate (do this gradually to keep mixture creamy, and do not add water to the concentrate).

• Stir in wafer crumbs. (Make crumbs by putting wafers into a blender. Or place wafers on a sheet of waxed paper, cover with another sheet of waxed paper, and move a rolling pin over the cookies, crushing them.)

• Using your hands, roll into one-inch balls.

• Pour coconut into a large bowl. Roll the balls in the coconut (or, for variety, you could also use chopped nuts).

• Makes four dozen balls.

Not-for-Breakfast Cornflake Candy

Ingredients

3 tablespoons butter or margarine
1 cup light brown sugar
⅓ cup evaporated milk
5 cups cornflakes (or other breakfast cereal—
assorted cold cereals may be used in
combination)
½ cup chopped nuts (optional)

Cooking Directions

• Melt the butter or margarine over low heat. Add sugar and stir constantly until sugar is dissolved. Continue stirring and slowly add evaporated milk.

• Keep the heat low as you add cereal and nuts. Mix thoroughly. Remove from heat.

• Press mixture into a greased, foil-lined 9-inch-by-9-inch pan. Cover with waxed paper and let stand in a cool, dry place.

• Break into pieces and serve like candy.

No-Bake Peanut Butter Balls

Ingredients

½ cup wheat germ
1 ½ cups peanut butter
1 ½ cups honey
3 cups dried milk powder
¾ cup graham cracker crumbs
(These are sold, ready to use, in a box, or you can take whole graham crackers and crumble them just as you did the vanilla wafers on page 42.)
2 cups confectioners' sugar

Cooking Directions

• Mix all ingredients, except confectioners' sugar, together thoroughly.

• Form into balls the size of large marbles.

• Place the confectioners' sugar in a large bowl and roll each ball in it until coated.

• Makes about five dozen little balls.

Use-Your-Noodle Cookies

Ingredients

1 six-ounce package of semisweet chocolate chips
1 six-ounce package of butterscotch chips
1 six-ounce can of salted peanuts
1 five-ounce can of Chinese chow mein noodles

Cooking Directions

• Melt chocolate and butterscotch chips together in top of double boiler (this is a pot that rests on another pot, which is filled with water to prevent burning). Stir from time to time, until all the chips are totally melted and blended.

• Remove from stove. Stir in peanuts and noodles.

• Drop from a teaspoon onto a wax-paper-covered cookie sheet. No more cooking is involved, but you should wait a few minutes until the cookies harden a bit before you eat them.

• Makes about three dozen crunchy cookies.

THREE

Sweet Valentine

One December morning, there was a visitor in Mrs. Cheechia's classroom. It was her son Greg, who was an eighth grader at Mark Twain Junior High School. His school's furnace had broken down, and the school was closed for the day.

It was the first time Cricket had ever seen a child of one of her teachers. Greg Cheechia was tall and dark-haired. Cricket thought he was so good-looking he should be on TV or in the movies.

Mrs. Cheechia asked Greg to help her distribute the spelling quizzes that she'd marked the night before.

"Cricket Kaufman?" he called out.

Cricket blushed and raised her hand.

"That's a cute name you have," he commented, and her heart flip-flopped.

For once Cricket was hardly aware that she had

a perfect paper. She was much busier thinking about Greg Cheechia. She wondered if he thought she was cute, like her name. And she wondered if he had noticed her grade. If he had, she hoped he'd been impressed.

Later Mrs. Cheechia had her son sit next to Carol Simmons and help her by going over yesterday's math homework. Poor Carol always seemed about a month behind her classmates in math. But today Cricket envied her. If only she needed extra help too! Then Greg Cheechia would be sitting next to her.

By the end of the school day, Cricket realized that she was falling in love with Greg Cheechia. It had never happened to her before, but it was no wonder. Who could fall in love with the boys who were in her class? Lucas Cott? Julio Sanchez? Arthur Lewis? None of them had the wonderful smile of Greg Cheechia. These days Arthur had braces that made him look as if he'd tried to swallow his mother's tableware. Julio was shorter than Cricket since her latest growth spurt. And as for Lucas, forget about it. No one but his mother could love Lucas Cott.

Cricket raised her hand. "Will Greg come back another time?" she asked Mrs. Cheechia shyly.

The teacher looked at her son. "How would you like to come to our class Christmas party?" she suggested to him.

"Sure," said Greg, smiling. "I love parties."

Cricket thought he probably also liked being older and bigger and smarter than all the kids in his mother's class. And maybe, just maybe, he liked Cricket and wanted to come back to see her again.

The Christmas party was held on the last afternoon before the school vacation. The plan was for everyone to bring a treat to eat. Even though she'd been doing a lot of cooking lately, Cricket had trouble deciding what to bring. She wanted something that would really appeal to Greg Cheechia, something different and special. She hunted through all her mother's cookbooks to find just the right thing to make. So when she saw a recipe for cookies called Sweet Kisses, she knew that was perfect.

Cricket came to school on the morning of the Christmas party wearing a new red sweater. She wanted to be sure Greg noticed her. All during the party she watched Greg, though of course she was careful that neither he nor her classmates were aware of that. Still, it was hard not to break out into a huge grin when she saw him stuff three Sweet Kisses into his mouth. Of course, she noticed, he had many pieces of just about every dessert that was offered. It must be because he was bigger than the sixth graders and needed more nourishment than they did. If she'd eaten that much of everything, she'd have exploded right there in the classroom.

When they were all putting on their jackets and caps to go home, Greg said, "Have a great holiday, Cricket." She was thrilled that he remembered her name. But she was even more excited when she turned to get one last look at him as she was walking out of the classroom and he winked at her.

Cricket replayed the memory of that wink for days and days. It was like rewinding a video on the VCR and watching her favorite part over and over.

For several weeks, Cricket kept her feelings for Greg Cheechia a secret. She didn't want anyone laughing at her just because she liked the teacher's son. Her mother would probably say that she should find a boyfriend who was her own age. But Cricket knew that she was mature for her age and so it only made sense that she'd be attracted to an older boy. Since he was in eighth grade, Greg was probably almost fourteen!

A month passed, and Cricket wondered if she would ever get to see Greg again. But there was an actor on one of her favorite TV shows who resembled Greg, and whenever she saw him, she thought of her teacher's handsome son. When stores began advertising for Valentine's Day, Cricket got the idea of sending him a card for the holiday. She had already looked in the telephone book, and there was only one family named Cheechia listed. So she had the address. The next thing she had to decide was whether or not she would sign the card. Greg might guess it was from her even without her signature, she thought.

One day in early February, she stopped in Harper's Party Shop together with Zoe. Zoe was buying a birthday card to give her mother. Cricket helped Zoe make up her mind which card to select. Then the two girls walked over to the display of valentine cards. They read some of them aloud to each other and giggled at the funny ones.

"Did you ever get a valentine?" Cricket asked Zoe.

"I get one every year from my stepfather," Zoe said. "He sends one to my sister and one to my mother too."

"I mean, did you ever get a card from a *boy,*" Cricket said.

"Before I moved here, in my old school, I got two cards. But whoever sent them didn't sign them, and I never figured out who they were from."

"Did you ever send a valentine to anyone?" Cricket asked.

"Well, since my stepfather sends one to me, I usually send him one too," Zoe admitted.

"That doesn't count," said Cricket. "I mean did you ever send a card to a boy our age? Or a little bit older?"

Zoe shook her head no. "What about you?" she asked.

Cricket shook her head too. She wondered if she should tell Zoe how she felt about Greg. After all, Zoe was her best friend.

As they left the store, Cricket said slowly, "I think I may send a valentine to someone this year."

"Who?" Zoe asked at once. "Is it someone I know?"

"Well, it's someone you've met," said Cricket.

"Someone in our class?"

"Not exactly," said Cricket.

"What does that mean?" Zoe wanted to know. "Either someone's in our class or they're not in our class. Do you mean he was in our class last year? Peter? Franklin?" She paused a moment, thinking of who else had been with them in fifth grade.

"They're babies," said Cricket. "The person I'm thinking of is older than we are."

"But all the boys in sixth grade are just about the same age," said Zoe, looking puzzled.

"This isn't someone in sixth grade," Cricket explained mysteriously.

"If he's not in sixth grade, then he can't be in our class," Zoe pointed out.

"Exactly," said Cricket.

"Cricket Kaufman, tell me right now. It's only fair. I'd tell you if I was going to send a valentine to someone," Zoe said.

"Promise you won't tell anyone?" Cricket asked her.

"Of course," said Zoe. "You know you can trust me."

"I was thinking of sending a card to Greg Cheechia," Cricket said, half whispering.

"Ooooh. Do you like him?" asked Zoe.

Cricket shrugged her shoulders. "Well, I sort of think he's cute," she said.

"Oh, you *do* like him. I can tell," said Zoe. "He's in my sister Halley's class at the junior high. He's even been to my house a couple of times. They were doing a science project together, and he came over when they were working on it."

"Greg Cheechia was at your house, and you never even told me?" Cricket asked. If only she had known, she could have gone over to visit Zoe when Greg was there.

"It was no big deal," said Zoe. "They just sat around talking about science stuff."

Cricket looked at Zoe. "Promise me that if he comes over to your house again, you'll call me right away."

"I promise," said Zoe. She gave Cricket's hand a squeeze. "If you want, tomorrow I'll go to Harper's with you again and I'll help you pick out a good card to send him."

The next day it took Cricket and Zoe almost an hour to select the perfect card. They read dozens of them aloud to each other.

"I don't think I should send a mushy card like this," said Cricket. "'My heart sings and the world is full of music when you are near me,'" she read aloud.

"Oh no. That's terrible," responded Zoe. She sang the words of the card, and both girls started giggling.

Cricket pulled another card off the rack. "I better get a funny card," she said. "This one's kind of cute," she observed. The card showed two bears walking hand in hand. The message inside read "I can't bear to be without you."

What appealed to Cricket was that the girl bear was wearing a red sweater like the one she was wearing the last time she and Greg were together.

"This is the perfect one," Cricket decided. "I'm going to buy it!"

The card cost a dollar and a half, which she thought was an awful lot of money for a piece of paper with such a short message on it. Still, Greg Cheechia was worth it, she told herself.

Cricket addressed the envelope carefully in her neatest cursive writing. After changing her mind back and forth, she'd finally decided not to sign her name. She considered drawing a tiny picture of a cricket at the bottom of the card but decided against it. It would give away who she was, and besides, she wasn't certain that she could actually draw a cricket. It might look more like just any old bug.

And then something awful happened. Only an hour after Cricket had mailed her valentine card to Greg Cheechia, Zoe phoned her. "I have to tell you something terrible," Zoe said.

"What is it?" asked Cricket.

"Promise that you won't get upset?" Zoe said.

"How can I promise when I don't know what you're going to tell me?" Cricket protested. "Besides, you already said that it was terrible."

"Well, promise anyhow," said Zoe. "Otherwise, I'm not going to tell you."

Cricket promised only because she was so curious about what it was that Zoe wanted to tell her. And then she was sorry that she had, because Zoe's news was more than just terrible. It was terrible, horrible, and heartbreaking.

"Greg Cheechia invited my sister Halley's friend Cheryl to the valentine dance at the junior high school. Halley says he took Cheryl to the movies last weekend too. According to Halley, they're in a serious relationship."

Suddenly, all the joy of Cricket's secret love collapsed like a deflating balloon. Greg Cheechia would just throw her valentine card in the garbage. He wouldn't know who sent it and he wouldn't care. He would be too busy thinking about that other girl, Cheryl.

Cricket got off the phone and went into her bedroom. She lay down on her bed with her shoes on. She knew her mother would be annoyed if she saw that, but for once Cricket didn't care. So what if she got the quilt dirty? What did it matter? Nothing mattered. Greg Cheechia liked a girl named Cheryl. He didn't like her. Probably no one would ever like her.

A little later Mrs. Kaufman knocked on Cricket's door. "Honey, I almost forgot. You got a piece of mail today. I put it in my pocketbook because I met the mail carrier as I was about to drive off in the car."

Cricket jumped off her bed and opened the door. Her mother handed her a white envelope.

Cricket looked at the envelope. Her name and address had been printed in ink, and the stamp had been pasted on upside down. Cricket ripped the flap open. Inside there was a card with a big red heart surrounded by flowers and birds and the words *To My Valentine.* Cricket had seen the card before. It was one of the cards that she had seen and rejected at Harper's Party Shop because it had

seemed too mushy. Inside, the printed message read,

Flowers would lose their color,
Birds would lose their song.
Nothing in life would matter
If you were not along.

Underneath those words the sender had added *I hope you will be my sweatheart.*

Cricket turned bright red. Someone had sent her a card. Someone liked her, even if Greg Cheechia didn't. Whoever it was had even pasted the stamp on upside down. Everyone knew that an upside-down stamp meant "I love you." She wondered who had sent the card. Because the message, like her name and address, was printed, she couldn't use the handwriting to figure out who her secret admirer was. It had to be one of the boys in her class. Lucas? Julio? Arthur? She didn't think she liked any of them. Still, it was nice to know that someone cared about her. Someone. Who?

The more Cricket thought about it, the more she found herself hoping the card had been sent by Lucas. Lucas could be a real pain sometimes. He was always making jokes and fooling around.

But on the other hand, he was much better than he used to be. The old Lucas Cott had been terrible. But the new Lucas Cott, the sixth grader, sometimes said very clever things in class. He was really quite smart. Of course, he wasn't as smart as she was, but he probably was the smartest boy in their class. Also, come to think of it, with his blond hair and blue eyes, he wasn't bad-looking.

It wasn't until Cricket looked at the card for the fourth or fifth time that she realized that the word *sweetheart* was misspelled as *sweatheart.* That could be a clue, she thought. She wondered about the spelling skills of the different boys in her class. Lucas Cott would never make a silly mistake like that.

All through supper and as she practiced for her piano lesson and as she did her homework, a part of Cricket's brain concentrated on her mysterious boyfriend. Arthur was an atrocious speller. Cricket could remember back in second grade, when he even spelled his own name wrong: He kept writing *Aurthr* on his papers. Nowadays, of course, he knew how to spell his name. But did he know how to spell *sweetheart*? Probably not. Cricket put down her pencil. She knew that as much as she complained about Lucas, she'd much rather that her valentine be from him than from Arthur.

Then a wonderful thought came to her. Lucas Cott was so smart that he'd know she would guess he sent the card. So he must have deliberately misspelled a word so she wouldn't think he'd sent the valentine. Lucas sure was clever, she thought, smiling to herself. But the truth was, no matter how clever he was, she was even smarter. Maybe I'll tell Zoe, Cricket thought. But I'll never tell Lucas, she decided.

Quickly Cricket finished her homework assignment. Then, when she could bear it no longer, she went to the phone. She didn't call Zoe.

She dialed the number of Lucas Cott.

"Hi, Lucas," she said to him.

"Hi," Lucas responded.

"We haven't done any cooking in a long time," Cricket reminded him. "I was thinking that it would be fun to cook something *sweet* together. Do you want to come over on Saturday? We could make some kind of cookies or cake or even candy."

"Sure," Lucas agreed readily. "That sounds great. My mother says I've got a real sweet tooth. But I think all my teeth are sweet. Could we make fudge?"

"I'll look in our cookbooks. Maybe I'll find something different. Something you haven't tried before."

"Great," said Lucas. "I'll tell Julio. And you tell Zoe and Sara Jane. We always have a lot of fun when we cook together."

For a moment Cricket was disappointed that Lucas wanted their classmates to join them. You'd think that if he liked her, he would want to spend some time with her *alone.* But then she realized that it was really clever of Lucas to say that. If he was going to be her secret boyfriend, he needed to have other people around to cover up how he really felt.

"Okay," said Cricket. "You call Julio."

And then Lucas really blew his cover.

"No sweat," he said.

Sweet Kisses

Ingredients

2 egg whites, at room temperature
⅛ teaspoon salt
⅛ teaspoon cream of tartar
½ cup sugar
1 cup chopped walnuts or chocolate chips (optional)

Cooking Directions

• Preheat oven to 300 degrees.

• In bowl, beat egg whites with an electric mixer. (Or use an eggbeater and a lot of energy if you don't have a mixer.) Add salt and cream of tartar; continue beating until egg whites are

very foamy and begin to thicken. Add sugar a little at a time and beat well each time after each addition.

• When egg whites are very stiff, add walnuts or chocolate chips, if desired. Drop by teaspoons onto greased baking sheets. Bake for 25 minutes.

• Turn off oven and open oven door slightly. Cool kisses in oven; when completely cool, remove from baking sheets.

• Makes about three dozen kisses.

"Be My Honey" Cookies

Ingredients

1 stick butter or margarine, at room temperature
½ cup white sugar
½ cup honey
1 egg
2 cups sifted flour
½ teaspoon salt
1 teaspoon ginger
1 teaspoon cinnamon
1 teaspoon baking soda
1 egg white, slightly beaten
¾ cup finely chopped salted peanuts

Cooking Directions

- Preheat oven to 350 degrees.

• Mix butter or margarine, sugar, and honey together in a bowl until light and fluffy. Add egg and beat well.

• Sift flour, salt, ginger, cinnamon, and baking soda together into separate bowl. Add to honey mixture and mix well.

• Drop dough by level tablespoons onto greased baking sheets. Flatten cookies with bottom of glass; brush with beaten egg white and sprinkle with chopped peanuts. Bake for 12 to 15 minutes.

• Makes about 3 dozen cookies.

Chocolate Truffles

Ingredients

¾ cup butter (one and a half sticks)
¾ cup unsweetened cocoa powder
1 can (14 ounces) condensed milk
(do not use evaporated milk)
1 tablespoon vanilla extract
¾ cup cocoa powder or confectioners' sugar
or finely chopped nuts

Cooking Directions

- In a saucepan, melt butter over low heat.
- Add cocoa. Stir until smooth.
- Blend in condensed milk; stir constantly until

mixture is thick, smooth, and shiny. This takes about four minutes.

• Remove from heat; stir in vanilla.

• Chill in refrigerator for three to four hours or until firm.

• Shape into small balls; roll balls in cocoa or confectioners' sugar or chopped nuts. You can buy miniature muffin cups in which to place each chocolate truffle ball, and they will look very elegant when you serve them.

• Chill until firm. Store, covered, in refrigerator.

• If you didn't cheat and eat as you were working, and if you make the balls small, you should have about 30 chocolate truffles.

"Let's Make a Date" Nut Squares

Ingredients

2 eggs
½ cup sugar
½ teaspoon vanilla extract
½ cup flour
½ teaspoon baking powder
½ teaspoon salt
1 cup chopped walnuts
2 cups finely chopped dates
1 tablespoon confectioners' sugar, for sprinkling

Cooking Directions

- Preheat oven to 325 degrees.

- In a bowl, beat eggs until they are foamy. Add sugar and vanilla and blend well.

- In a second bowl, mix flour, baking powder, and salt. Stir into egg mixture. Add walnuts and dates and blend well.

- Spread batter in well-greased, 8-inch-square pan. Bake for 25 to 30 minutes. While still warm, cut into squares.

- Remove from pan. Put confectioners' sugar in a small strainer and shake over the squares to dust them with the sugar.

- Makes 16 squares.

FOUR

April Food's Day

It was an ordinary math class, of all things, that led Cricket and her classmates to begin planning an extraordinary party for their teacher.

It was all because the sixth graders were having a lesson in probability one day in March. Everyone, including the teacher, wrote the number of the day of the month when their birthday fell on a piece of paper. What was the probability of two people being born on the same day of the month? When the numbers were tallied, it turned out that Mrs. Cheechia was the only person whose birthday fell on the first day of the month.

"Not just any month," she told the students. "It's *April* first."

So one day late in March, the sixth graders began talking about making a party for their teacher.

"I bet it's fun to have your birthday on April

Fools' Day," commented Julio. "You could tell your friends that you're not having a party and then fool them by making a party after all."

"Yes, but it could work the other way too," Lucas pointed out. "What if you invited your friends to a party on April first, and no one came because everyone thought it was an April Fools' joke and there wasn't really going to be any party?"

"Oh," said Julio thoughtfully. "Well, then you could eat as much cake and ice cream as you wanted."

"And get good and sick!" said Cricket.

"And besides, you'd be disappointed not to have your friends there with you," commented Zoe.

"And no presents from your friends either," Lucas agreed.

"What are we going to do about Mrs. Cheechia's birthday?" Cricket asked. "Should we give a party?"

"Should we buy her a gift?" added Lucas.

"Maybe she'll surprise us and make a party for herself," said Zoe. "Remember last year in fifth grade, when Mr. Flores brought his guitar to school on a Tuesday? And then he surprised us by giving out cookies and ice cream at two o'clock in the afternoon."

"Right," Julio responded. "It was the middle of January, and we couldn't figure out what we were celebrating." We didn't know until the end that it was Mr. Flores's birthday."

"Let's have a surprise party for Mrs. Cheechia," said Zoe.

"Let's make it an April Fools' Day surprise birthday party!" said Lucas.

"What's the difference?" asked Sara Jane.

"We could bring surprising foods," suggested Zoe.

"We could act in surprising ways," said Lucas. "We could all pretend we hadn't done our homework the night before. You know, things like that."

Cricket looked suspiciously at Lucas. Since when did he need an excuse to fool around? she wondered.

April first was a week away. The students whispered plans to one another in class.

"Could you make that zucchini pie?" Julio asked Cricket. "That's a good April Fools' joke."

"I like to try making new things," Cricket observed. "But there are probably other things we could make that would be surprises."

"All the food could be jokes," said Lucas.

"Did you ever see those peppermints that look like green peas?" Arthur asked. "The green peas are really mints, and they're sold mixed with tiny orange squares of candy that look like diced carrots. I'll bring a package of them."

"That's a great idea!" said Julio.

Cricket was pretty certain that she could find a new recipe that would have a surprise twist to it. If she couldn't get zucchini, she could make a carrot cake, for example. But maybe she could make something that would *really* fool everyone.

Soon the search for surprising recipes became competitive.

"I've found a perfectly super and surprising dessert recipe," Zoe bragged to Cricket. "You'll love it, but you won't know what's inside."

"Why won't you tell me? I won't give away the secret," begged Cricket. What were best friends for if not to share secrets?

"If I tell you, it won't be a surprise," Zoe explained. "I'll give you the recipe after the party. But I want you to be just as surprised as Mrs. Cheechia and everyone else in our class."

"Guess what?" Sara Jane told her friends. "I found a recipe for something called Gooseberry

Fool. Doesn't that sound like just the right thing to eat on April Fools' Day?"

"What are gooseberries?" Cricket asked. "I've never seen or eaten any."

"Me neither," Sara Jane confessed. "I thought maybe you would know where I could buy some gooseberries."

Cricket shook her head. "Don't ask me. You'll have to ask a goose," she said, giggling.

Sara Jane looked disappointed and didn't laugh at the joke.

Cricket kept checking out cookbooks from the library. "You must be quite a cook," the librarian observed when Cricket staggered out with six thick volumes of recipes.

Cricket smiled proudly. She was getting to be pretty clever in the kitchen these days. Maybe when she was president of the United States, she could cook dinners for all the heads of the other world powers. That would be a first, she thought.

Sure enough, Cricket's persistence paid off. One evening, going through still another cookbook, she discovered the perfect April Fools' cake. She wondered if it was the same thing that Zoe was making. She rushed to the phone and called her classmate.

"Does the April Fools' recipe that you're making for Mrs. Cheechia's birthday have a crazy ingredient in it?"

"What do you mean, crazy?" asked Zoe.

"You know. Something that no one would ever dream is inside a cake?"

Zoe thought for a moment. "Not really," she said. "Besides, what I'm making isn't exactly a cake."

"Cookies?" asked Cricket.

"No. Now don't ask me any more questions. I told you I want to keep the dessert I'm making a secret."

"That's okay," said Cricket. "I've got a great recipe myself."

Finally it was time to tear off the March page from the calendar. April first had arrived. All the class members had arranged with some of their teachers from years past to leave the boxes of goodies in their classrooms.

Cricket's head felt like it was about to burst with all the plans. Lucas had given her so many instructions about what to do and what to say. In the past she would never have paid any attention to what Lucas told her. But ever since she had received the unsigned valentine, which she was still convinced came from Lucas, she found she treated him a little bit more nicely than she used to.

"This is going to be fun." Sara Jane giggled as she took her seat.

Mrs. Cheechia walked into the classroom. Cricket took a deep breath and began moving her mouth up and down as if she were chewing a piece of gum. All around her the other students, instructed by Lucas, were doing the same thing. At first it didn't appear as if Mrs. Cheechia noticed anything. She hung her coat in the closet in the back of the room and walked toward her desk.

"Julio, are you chewing gum so early in the morning?" Mrs. Cheechia said.

Julio shook his head. "I'm not chewing any gum," he announced to the teacher. His mouth continued moving as before.

Mrs. Cheechia looked around the room. Every mouth was in motion, up and down. "What's going on here?" she asked. "Are you all chewing gum? You know that is one rule I strictly enforce in my class. All gum goes in the garbage can. Right now."

"April Fools'!" the children shouted in unison.

Mrs. Cheechia let out a gasp. "Well, you really

fooled me," the teacher admitted, smiling.

Cricket was glad that joke was over. Her jaws ached from all that pretend chewing. But there were lots of other jokes to come. When Mrs. Cheechia asked for the homework papers to be passed forward, the students sat motionless.

"Where are everyone's papers?" asked Mrs. Cheechia.

Lucas raised his hand. "I had to take care of my little brothers last night. So I couldn't do my homework."

Julio's hand went up next. "My grandmother was sick, and I had to take her to the doctor," he explained. "I couldn't do my homework either."

One by one the students gave their excuses. "I was too busy practicing the piano," said Cricket. She felt her face turning red as she recited her line.

"My gerbil ate my homework," said Arthur.

"My mother threw my homework in the garbage by mistake," said Zoe, trying to keep from smiling.

"My little brother scribbled all over it and then he tore it into little pieces," said someone else.

Mrs. Cheechia began laughing. By now she knew it was a joke. "Any other excuses?" she asked. "I must say, I'm very impressed with the power of your imaginations."

"My uncle took my homework to the North Pole," said one boy.

"My mother cooked it with the other ingredients for supper," said someone else.

Finally, when every single student had given a reason for not handing in his or her homework, Lucas stood up. It was the signal for everyone else to stand too. "April Fools'!" they shouted together.

Mrs. Cheechia was laughing so hard that there were tears in her eyes.

The students laughed too. It wasn't every day that they could make jokes with their teacher. They all sat down and located their homework pages to pass in. All except Arthur. "I got confused," he said. "I really thought we weren't going to do the homework last night."

"Oh, Arthur," moaned Cricket. "It was just a joke."

"April Fools'!" Arthur shouted. And suddenly he pulled his homework out of his desk. Not only had he fooled Mrs. Cheechia, he had fooled Cricket as well.

There were several other April Fools' jokes played by the students during the morning. They all gave the wrong answers on purpose during social studies, and they made silly "errors" during language arts time. Cricket found it quite exhausting trying to think of mistakes to make. She was a very good student, and the correct answers, like correct behavior, came naturally to her. Misbehaving and making mistakes were hard work!

Finally it was lunchtime. The students could hardly wait for lunch to be over. Mrs. Cheechia hadn't mentioned that it was her birthday, and none of the students had let on that they remembered. The biggest surprises were to take place in the afternoon.

When the students returned to their seats after lunch, Zoe raised her hand. "May I please be excused?" she asked.

"Zoe, why didn't you go to the girls' room during the lunch break?" asked Mrs. Cheechia.

Zoe just shrugged her shoulders.

Mrs. Cheechia sighed and handed her the pass to leave the room. When Zoe returned a few minutes later, she was holding a large flowerpot with a fake flower sticking up out of it.

Cricket thought it was just another April Fools' joke.

"Happy birthday, Mrs. Cheechia!" said Zoe.

Mrs. Cheechia looked surprised. "How did you know it was my birthday?" she asked.

"We all know," shouted Julio. "You told us."

"I did?" asked the teacher. "I guess I forgot about that."

"And we're having a party!" Lucas announced.

"We're *giving* you a party," Cricket said, correcting her classmate.

One by one, the students went off and collected the party fare. There were the candies that looked like peas and carrots, and there was a pineapple upside-down cake. Sara Jane had never found any gooseberries, so in the end she had made a carrot cake. Cricket was pleased with the mystery ingredient in her cake, but she wouldn't tell what it was. "Wait until you eat it, and then see if you can guess," she told her classmates.

Zoe's flowerpot turned out to be filled with not only a fake flower, but also fake dirt. The dirt was really a kind of chocolate pudding. There were even gummy worms inside. Cricket wished that she had thought to make something like that. Luckily, Zoe promised to teach her how. Maybe someday when Monica was a little bigger and had a birthday party, Cricket would make it for her.

APRIL
1
HAPPY
BIRTHDAY
MRS. CHEECHIA

The children sang "Happy Birthday" to their teacher and then loaded up their plates with the party foods.

"This certainly is a surprise," Mrs. Cheechia kept saying.

No one was able to guess the mystery ingredient in Cricket's cake. Julio said zucchini because it had been right the last time he had made a wild guess. This time he was wrong.

Sara Jane guessed eggs.

"That's not a mystery ingredient," said Cricket. "Almost all cakes have eggs."

"Potatoes?"

"Rice?"

"Buttermilk," guessed Mrs. Cheechia. Even she was wrong.

When everyone had ventured a guess and no one had come up with the correct answer, Cricket made her announcement. "The mystery ingredient is tomato soup," she said with triumph.

"I don't believe it," said Lucas. But it was not an April Fools' joke. It was the truth.

"All right, boys and girls," called Mrs. Cheechia when every crumb of cake and dirt had been consumed and all the peas and carrots had disappeared into the mouths of her students and all the paper plates and napkins had been put into the overflowing wastebasket. "Listen carefully while I give you your homework assignment."

"Homework?" the students moaned.

"Tonight?" demanded Julio. "You're giving us homework on Friday night?" The students rarely had homework assignments over the weekend.

"We have to make up for the time we lost this afternoon," said Mrs. Cheechia. "We didn't finish the science unit that we've been working on. I want you to read pages fifty-nine to seventy-five and answer all the questions at the end of the chapter."

"Aw, that's not fair," groaned Arthur, and his words were echoed by many of the students.

"It's not fair, but it's April Fools'!" called out Mrs. Cheechia as the dismissal bell rang. There was no homework after all.

The students left the school building laughing and commenting on the success of their party. "I loved baking that tomato soup cake," said Cricket to her friends.

"I still don't believe there was tomato soup in it," said Lucas. "I think you just made it up."

"Why don't you come to my house tomorrow, and we'll make another one," Cricket said to

Lucas. "Everyone come," she added, inviting Zoe, Sara Jane, Lucas, and Julio, who were all standing together.

"Is that an April Fools' joke or a real invitation?" Zoe asked.

"It's for real," Cricket said seriously. "I think we should start a club and cook together all the time. We always have fun when we cook."

"I second the motion!" shouted Julio.

"I even found another cake with a different mystery ingredient," Cricket told her friends. "It has mayonnaise in it, but it's a chocolate cake. I had a hard time deciding which cake to make for today. We'll have to try that one too."

"We won't cook asparagus or cabbage, will we?" asked Sara Jane. "I don't like them."

"Don't be silly," said Cricket. "Just desserts."

"Chocolate cake, apple pie, peanut butter cookies, and Zoe's dirt. Only the best," said Lucas.

"I second the motion!" Julio called out again.

"We'll even make Gooseberry Fool, if we ever find gooseberries," said Cricket.

"Just desserts. We'll have a great time," called out Zoe.

And that was no April Fools' joke.

Cricket's Souper Surprise Cake

Ingredients

2 cups all-purpose flour
½ teaspoon salt
1 teaspoon cinnamon
¼ teaspoon nutmeg
¼ teaspoon cloves
1 teaspoon baking soda
1 cup white sugar
2 tablespoons butter or margarine, at room temperature
1 can condensed tomato soup (do not add water)
1 cup chopped walnuts
1 cup raisins

Cooking Directions

• Preheat oven to 350 degrees.

• Measure out one cup of sugar into a bowl and add two tablespoons of butter or margarine. Mix together with a fork.

• Add all the dry ingredients: flour, salt, spices. Mix together.

• Add the condensed tomato soup to the other ingredients.

• Stir until smooth.

• Add walnuts and raisins.

• Bake in a greased and floured tube pan for about 45 minutes. Test for doneness by poking a wooden toothpick into cake. If it comes out dry, you will know the cake is ready to be removed from the oven.

• Cooled cake may be served plain or frosted. (See frosting recipe given with carrot cake.) Slices of plain cake could also be topped with freshly whipped sweetened cream.

Better-Than-17-Carat-Gold Carrot Cake

Cake Ingredients

4 eggs
2 cups of white sugar
1 ½ cups canola or corn oil
2 cups flour
2 teaspoons baking soda
½ teaspoon cinnamon
3 cups grated carrots
8-ounce can crushed pineapple
(chopped walnuts or pecans, optional)

Frosting Ingredients

8 ounces cream cheese, at room temperature

1 stick butter or margarine, at room temperature
2 teaspoons vanilla
1 sixteen-ounce box confectioners' sugar
½ cup raisins
½ cup chopped pecans

Cooking Directions

- Preheat oven to 350 degrees.
- Beat eggs and sugar together.
- Stir in oil. Add other ingredients. Mix thoroughly.
- Pour into greased and floured 10-inch-by-15-inch sheet pan.
- Bake for half an hour. Test for doneness with a wooden toothpick.
- While cake is cooling, make frosting by blending all frosting ingredients together. Spread on cooled cake.

Dirt

Ingredients

1 one-pound package chocolate sandwich cookies
8 ounces cream cheese at room temperature
1 stick butter or margarine, melted
1 cup confectioners' sugar
1 teaspoon vanilla
1 12-ounce container whipped dessert topping
2 packages instant chocolate pudding
3 cups milk

Cooking Directions

• Crush the cookies to the consistency of dirt. You could do this using a blender or by putting cookies between two sheets of waxed paper and crushing with a rolling pin.

• Mix the melted butter and cream cheese until smooth. Add confectioners' sugar. Fold in whipped topping.

• Mix the pudding with milk and vanilla and fold into above mixture.

• Line a brand-new flowerpot with aluminum foil. This will plug the hole in the bottom. Layer crushed cookies and pudding mixture into pot, ending with some crushed cookies on top. Gummy worms can be added for decoration (or surprise) and some plastic flowers can be stuck into pot for added effect.

• Serve with a clean trowel.

Mystery Ingredient Chocolate Cake

Ingredients

3 eggs
1 ⅔ cup sugar
1 teaspoon vanilla
1 cup mayonnaise
2 cups all-purpose flour
1 ¼ teaspoons baking soda
¼ teaspoon baking powder
⅔ cup unsweetened cocoa
1 ⅓ cups water

Cooking Directions

- Preheat oven to 350 degrees. Grease and

flour a 10-inch-by-15-inch sheet pan.

• Beat eggs with sugar. Add vanilla and mayonnaise and beat together.

• Add flour with baking soda, baking powder, and cocoa. Gradually add the water.

• Pour the batter into the prepared pan. Bake until a toothpick inserted in the center comes out clean—about 25 minutes. Cool.

• Serve with confectioners' sugar sprinkled through a strainer on top of the cake or with whipped cream or ice cream.

About the Author

JOHANNA HURWITZ is the award-winning author of many popular books for young readers, including *Starting School, Llama in the Library, Ever-Clever Elisa,* and *Faraway Summer.* She has received a number of child-chosen state awards, including the Texas Bluebonnet Award, the Kentucky Bluegrass Award, and the Garden State Children's Book Award. A former children's librarian, Mrs. Hurwitz travels around the country to visit schools and discuss books with students, teachers, parents, and librarians.

The author, a cooking enthusiast, once won first prize at a county fair in Vermont for her blackberry jam recipe. She also took top honors in a nationwide rice recipe competition sponsored by Uncle Ben's. Mrs. Hurwitz lives with her husband in Great Neck, New York, and Wilmington, Vermont.